AXLE ANNIE

Robin Pulver
pictures by Tedd Arnold

Dial Books for Young Readers ❖ New York

For my sister and brother-in-law, Claire and Dick
Damaske, who have helped me through storms so many
times before. Thanks a million!—*R.P.*

To Marvia and Paulette, with memories of snow—*T.A.*

———————————

Published by Dial Books for Young Readers
A division of Penguin Putnam Inc.
345 Hudson Street
New York, New York 10014
Text copyright © 1999 by Robin Pulver
Pictures copyright © 1999 by Tedd Arnold
All rights reserved
Designed by Nancy R. Leo-Kelly
Printed in Hong Kong
First Edition
1 3 5 7 9 10 8 6 4 2

Library of Congress Cataloging in Publication Data
Pulver, Robin.
Axle Annie/Robin Pulver; pictures by Tedd Arnold.—1st ed.
p.   cm.
Summary: The schools in Burskyville never close for snow, because
Axle Annie is always able to make it up the steepest hill in town,
until Shifty Rhodes and Hale Snow set out to stop her.
ISBN 0-8037-2096-3
[1. School buses—Fiction. 2. Snow—Fiction.]
I. Arnold, Tedd, ill. II. Title.
PZ7.P97325Ax 1999 [E]—dc21 98-8696 CIP AC

The artwork was prepared with colored pencils and watercolor washes.

IN THE TOWN OF BURSKYVILLE the luckiest kids rode on Axle Annie's school bus. Axle Annie did magic tricks. She told jokes and sang silly songs. The kids couldn't wait to see her every morning and hear her cheerful call, "Get on up these steps before I leave without you!"

Winter packed a wallop in Burskyville. Whenever a storm came up, the superintendent of schools, Mr. Solomon, telephoned Axle Annie.

"It's nasty out there, Annie!" he'd say. "Think you can make it up Tiger Hill? If you say no, I'll close the schools. My decision depends on you."

Tiger Hill was on Axle Annie's
bus route. It was the toughest hill in
Burskyville. But Axle Annie's reply was
always the same: "Mr. Solomon!
Do snowplows plow? Do tow trucks tow?
Are school buses yellow? Of course
I can make it up Tiger Hill!"
    And she always did. That's
why the schools in Burskyville
never had a snow day.

Shifty Rhodes *hated* that. Shifty was the nastiest school bus driver in Burskyville. At every meeting of the Grouch and Grump Club, Shifty complained about his job. Especially in winter! He grumbled about having to get up early to warm up his bus. He fussed about trucks sloshing slush all over his windshield. He bellyached about boots that made puddles on the bus. "And I never ever get a snow day!" he always said. "All because of that Axle Annie."

One rip-roaring winter morning Axle Annie's phone rang. "It's a blizzard out there, Annie!" the superintendent said. "Think you can make it up Tiger Hill? If you say no, I'll close the schools. My decision depends on you."

"Mr. Solomon," Axle Annie replied, "do snowplows plow? Do tow trucks tow? Are school buses yellow? Of course I can make it up Tiger Hill!"

Shifty Rhodes was still in bed.

"And now for the school closings," announced his radio. "Every town in the five-county area has closed its schools except for one. And that's—"

"Don't say Burskyville!" pleaded Shifty.

"Burskyville," said the radio.

"All because of Axle Annie," grumbled Shifty. He bundled up and headed for his bus .

Axle Annie was already on her way. When Tiger Hill loomed ahead, she called out, "Hold on to your earmuffs!"

"Gun the engine!" shouted the kids. "Put your pedal to the metal!" Axle Annie did. And she roared up Tiger Hill, past all the ditched vehicles and stranded drivers.

At the top she stopped, as usual, and called back to the snowbound drivers,
"Get on up these steps before I leave without you!" They rode along with the kids
to school, where they telephoned for tow trucks to pull their cars out of the snow.

Of course Shifty Rhodes was in a terrible mood that morning. When the kids on his bus got the least bit noisy, he yelled, "You drive me crazy!"

And the kids yelled back, "You're the one that's driving. Not us!"

Shifty was still mad when he ventured out that night to the
Grouch and Grump Club. But then a miracle happened.
A new member introduced himself: "The name's Hale Snow.
Snow's my name and snow's my game."

Hale explained that he was the new owner of the Burskyville Ski Resort. "Business is bad," he grumbled. "I even bought a new snowmaking machine, but who needs it? It just sits on my truck like a bamboozled bump on a blizzard-blasted log. The best days for me should be snow days, when kids head for the slopes because school's closed. But the snow-blasted schools here never close!"

After the meeting Shifty Rhodes collared Hale Snow. "You know why we never get a snow day?" he asked. "Axle Annie! That's why!" And Shifty told Hale all about Axle Annie and Tiger Hill.

"Snarlin' snowflakes!" exclaimed Hale. "There must be something we can do!"

"Maybe there is," said Shifty. "With that snowmaking machine of yours . . ."

"I get your drift," said Hale. "Just say the word, and I'll haul my machine over to Tiger Hill. We'll whomp up such a storm there, not even Axle Annie will make it up the hill."

"Whoop-de-do!" cheered Shifty.

The very next Monday morning Axle Annie's telephone rang.

"Annie!" said Mr. Solomon. "It's the storm of the century! Think you can make it up Tiger Hill? If you say no, I'll close the schools. My decision depends on you."

"Mr. Solomon," replied Axle Annie, "do snowplows plow? Do tow trucks tow? Are school buses yellow? Of course I can make it up Tiger Hill!"

Meanwhile, Shifty Rhodes was peering outside into howling whiteness. "Yippee!" he shouted, and telephoned Hale Snow. "No school in its right mind should be open today."

"It's a wingdinger of a storm!" Hale agreed. "And my machine will make it ten times as bad on Tiger Hill. Axle Annie will never make it up. Meet me there and watch the fun for yourself."

Icy snow stung Shifty's face as he plodded to his bus. Finally he revved up the engine and drove into the storm.

Shifty's bus slithered and slid its way to Tiger Hill. Suddenly Shifty caught sight of something in the road. He leaned on the brakes, but the bus skidded and bucked and plowed right into whatever it was.

"Sled-bustin' snowflakes, Shifty!" hollered Hale Snow. "You clobbered my snowmaking machine!"

Shifty apologized, but he couldn't feel too bad. Hale Snow's machine had turned Tiger Hill into a monstrous mountain of swirling snow!

As Axle Annie's bus approached Tiger Hill, the kids yelled, "Yikes!"
"Hold on to your earmuffs!" Annie called.
"Gun the engine, Annie!" shouted the kids. "Put the pedal to the metal."
Axle Annie tried. But near the top of the snowy hill, the wheels spun. The
engine strained. The bus was stuck.
"You can do it, Annie!" the kids yelled. But for the first time ever, Annie
wasn't sure she could. Would the Burskyville schools close after all?

Then suddenly the bus seemed to sprout wings!
Slowly and gently it glided up, up, up to the top of Tiger Hill.

"HOORAY!" shouted the kids. Axle Annie looked around. It wasn't wings that she saw. It was all the stranded drivers that Annie had helped so many times before!

"Thanks a million," shouted Annie. "Now get on up these steps before I leave without you!"

Then Annie looked again and saw two snowmen trudging up the hill: Shifty Rhodes and Hale Snow. When Annie saw the mangled snowmaking machine down below, their whole mean plot came to her in a flash.

Axle Annie gunned her engine. But Shifty and Hale looked so miserable, she couldn't be mad. "Oh, get on up these steps," she called.

"Before we leave without you!" yelled the kids.

Shifty Rhodes had to pay all the money in his piggy bank to fix his school bus and the snowmaking machine. Then he skedaddled out of town and got a job on a cruise ship.

Hale Snow was sorry he'd ever gotten mixed up with Shifty Rhodes. He thought Axle Annie was one humdinger of a woman. In fact, his business doubled when he named a new ski slope after her.

AXLE ANNIE
◆ SLOPE ◆

Whenever kids headed for that steep and scary slope, they asked each other, "Think we can make it down okay?"

The answer was always the same: "Do snowplows plow? Do tow trucks tow? Are school buses yellow? Of course we can make it down Axle Annie Slope!"

And they USUALLY did.